We Came from Vietnam

Muriel Stanek

Photographs by **Wm. Franklin McMahon**

Albert Whitman & Company
Morton Grove, Illinois

Text © 1985 by Muriel Stanek.
Photographs © 1985 by Albert Whitman & Company.
Published by Albert Whitman & Company,
6340 Oakton Street, Morton Grove, Illinois 60053.
Published simultaneously in Canada by
General Publishing, Limited, Toronto.
All rights reserved. Printed in the U.S.A.
10   9   8   7   6   5   4   3

Library of Congress Cataloging in Publication Data

Stanek, Muriel.
  We came from Vietnam.

  SUMMARY: Text and black-and-white photographs describe
the efforts of a Vietnamese refugee family to adjust to
life in Chicago.

  1. Vietnamese Americans—Illinois—Chicago—Biography
—Juvenile literature. 2. Vietnamese Americans—Illinois
—Chicago—Portraits. 3. Vietnamese Americans—Illinois—
Chicago—Cultural assimilation—Juvenile literature.
4. Chicago (Ill.)—Foreign population—Juvenile literature.
5. Chicago (Ill.)—Biography—Portraits. [1. Vietnamese
Americans. 2. United States—Emigration and immigration.]
I. McMahon, William Franklin, ill.   II. Title.
F548.9.V53S73   1985   977.3'110049592   84-29927
ISBN 0-8075-8699-4

With special gratitude to the Xuan Thanh Nguyen family; the Stewart School of Chicago, Illinois; and Diane Le, bilingual teacher.

Thanks also to:
Louis Berkman, Vietnamese Community Service Center, Chicago, Illinois
Julius Hovany, Illinois Department of Commerce and Community Affairs
Ngoan Le, Vietnamese Association of Illinois
Bang Hai Nguyen, Quang Minh Vietnamese Buddhist Temple, Chicago, Illinois
Porter Reed, Office of Bilingual Education, Illinois State Board of Education
Dr. Patricia M. Ryan, Principal, Stewart School
Trang Ton, Vietnamese Community Service Center, Chicago, Illinois
Duong Tran, Truman College, Chicago, Illinois

Everyone in the Nguyen family has a name with a special meaning. The older son is Tuan Anh, meaning "famous person." The younger son is Tu Anh, meaning "bright and intelligent." The older daughter is Tuyen Thanh, meaning "gentle river." And the younger daughter is Loan, or "great beauty." Vietnamese parents hope their children will live up to their names.

Vietnamese names are written in reverse order of American names. The personal name is last, and the family name is first. In Vietnam, the father's full name was Nguyen Thanh Xuan, and he was called Mr. Xuan. But in America, his name is Xuan Thanh Nguyen, and he is Mr. Nguyen. His personal name, *Xuan*, means "prime of youth." Mrs. Nguyen's name in America is Giao Kim Nguyen. *Giao Kim* means "strong metal."

There are only about thirty family names for all Vietnamese. The most common is *Nguyen*, used by almost half the population. However, not all people with the same family name are related to one another.

The Nguyen children and their parents live in Chicago, a big, busy city in the United States. But this was not always their home. Once they lived on the other side of the world, in a village in Vietnam.

Vietnam is just south of China, in Southeast Asia, almost nine thousand miles by plane from Chicago (roughly three times the distance from New York to San Francisco). It is about the size of the state of New Mexico.

UPI/Bettmann

The shape of Vietnam is said to look a little like a bamboo carrying pole with a basket of rice balancing at each end. The imaginary rice baskets are the rich lands near the mouths of the Red River in the north and the Mekong River in the south. The imaginary pole is the narrow mountain range connecting these fertile river deltas.

The village the Nguyens came from is in the Mekong River delta. Farmers in this area work in the fields with simple equipment such as bamboo poles and baskets.

Mr. Nguyen was the manager of a small sugar factory. The family lived in a house that they owned, with Mr. Nguyens' parents and his unmarried sisters. Usually three generations of a Vietnamese family live together in the household of the oldest adult son. Most of the Nguyens' other relatives lived and worked nearby. Vietnamese families like to stay close together.

Long ago most of Vietnam was ruled by China. After many wars, the Vietnamese got their independence. They set up their own government more than a thousand years ago. But in the 1880s, the French took control of all of what is now Vietnam. There were more years of war before Vietnam got its independence again, in 1954. Then it was divided into two parts—North Vietnam and South Vietnam. Each part had its own government. The North Vietnamese government was Communist. The South Vietnamese government was against the Communists.

Within a few years, Communist fighters, known as the Vietcong, began attacking villages in South Vietnam. On the request of the South Vietnamese government, the United States sent military advisors to train South Vietnamese troops. The fighting grew worse. The United States began to send supplies and large numbers of soldiers to help defend South Vietnam against the Communists. Many Americans as well as Vietnamese were killed.

Finally, an agreement was signed to stop the fighting between the two Vietnams. The United States forces left. But soon North Vietnam brought in more troops. Saigon, the capital city of South Vietnam, fell into Communist hands in 1975. South Vietnam surrendered. In 1976, the Communists united North and South Vietnam into one country, known as Vietnam. The name of Saigon was changed to Ho Chi Minh City, after the revolutionary leader and former president of North Vietnam, Ho Chi Minh.

Now people had to work under the rules of the new government. Leaders of the old government were put into prison. Children were taught Communism in the schools, and adults had to attend night classes on Communism. Often people were forced by the government to take new jobs. Some were arrested when they did not do as the Communists demanded.

There was not enough food. Much of the farmland had been ruined by the war, and many farmers had deserted the land in search of safety. There were feelings of fear everywhere, and some people began leaving the country.

The Nguyen family wanted to leave, too. They wanted to go to the United States of America, where they believed they would have freedom. "Life will be like a ladder in America," said Mr. Nguyen to his family. "We will climb up, up, up to the top. If we stay in Vietnam now, we will be on a slide and go down, down, down. We must get to America."

But it was hard to get out of the country. Paper money, coins, or gold were needed to pay for transportation.

Then, in 1982, Mr. Nguyen's father gave him the family savings to pay for their boat trip. It was hard for the Nguyens to leave their home and relatives. They did not know if they would survive the trip or see one another again.

The Nguyens started out with Mrs. Nguyen's brother and his family in a small fishing boat. There were many more people in this boat, too. Some had to stand because it was so crowded. For days they wondered if they would ever reach a safe place.

At around the same time, thousands of other Vietnamese were leaving the country in different boats. Together, they became known as "the boat people." They were in great danger during their escape. Many drowned in the South China Sea. Some were turned away by countries that did not want them. Others had their money and boats stolen by sea pirates.

The Nguyen family and their relatives were among the lucky ones. They arrived safely at a camp for refugees in Thailand, a country close to Vietnam, in Southeast Asia. (Refugees are people who flee from their home country to find another home.)

All the Nguyens had with them were the clothes they wore. There was no shelter in the camp to protect them from the hot sun or rain. So they used branches and leaves to make a tent. They slept on the ground because there were no beds. There were no hospitals, medicine, doctors, or even running water. Life in the camp was especially hard on children and old people.

Later the Nguyens were moved to two other camps, set up by the United Nations. These camps were large and crowded. It was hard living in them, too. Food was scarce. What there was, mostly rice and fish, came from the Red Cross. The Nguyens waited month after month as other people left for different countries around the world. Their dream of going to America helped them to be brave.

After a year of waiting, it was the Nguyens' turn to leave. A church group in America helped them and other families come to the United States. A big 747 jet brought them to America from Southeast Asia.

The moment they saw the Chicago skyline, the Nguyens knew the United States was everything they hoped it would be. "It is a big, strong country," said Mrs. Nguyen. "It is new and modern. This will be a wonderful place for our children."

When the plane landed at O'Hare Airport, they felt they had at last reached the country of their dreams.

But soon there were new problems. It was hard to find a place to live. Everything cost too much. All they could afford was a small apartment in a crowded Chicago community called "Uptown." The apartment seemed even smaller when Mr. Nguyen's aunt and uncle later joined them from Vietnam.

Mrs. Nguyen's brother and his family moved into the apartment next door.

Uptown is busy and noisy. The streets are jammed with bus, truck, and automobile traffic. Loud trains go by on elevated tracks. People live close together in large apartment buildings. There is hardly a tree or blade of grass anywhere. Uptown is very different from the Nguyens' village in Vietnam, with its quiet country roads and open, green spaces. Their new neighbors come from many racial and ethnic backgrounds and speak many different languages.

At first the children and their parents spoke only to other Vietnamese who were their neighbors. Soon they found out that they needed to learn English so that they could make their way around the city, find jobs, read the newspaper and signs, and understand the television and radio.

Although English and Vietnamese have almost the same alphabet, they are very different. English is hard for many Vietnamese to learn because it has lots of long words. In Vietnamese most words have only one syllable. Many English words are also hard because they change form. In Vietnamese, words do not change form.

> English: Today I *pick* one *apple*.
> Vietnamese: Today I *pick* one *apple*.

> English: Yesterday I *pick**ed*** two *apple**s***.
> Vietnamese: Yesterday I *pick* two *apple*.

But Vietnamese is also hard for native English-speaking people to learn. It has six different tones, like notes on a scale. Because of the different tones, spoken Vietnamese sounds a little like singing. Marks are written by some letters to show the correct tone for each word. Often these marks are all that makes one word or name different from another. For example, *hòa* (said in a low, falling tone) means "peace," and *hoa* (said in a normal, even tone) means "flower."

Mr. and Mrs. Nguyen began taking English lessons at a nearby community college. Other people new to the United States were in their class. They came from many different countries. All of them wanted to become American citizens.

It was a happy day when the Nguyen children started public school. Education is very important to the Vietnamese. Educated people hold an honored place among them, and teachers are greatly respected.

In Vietnam, education is free and required for all children from age six through the first five primary grades.

If the Nguyens had stayed in Vietnam, the children would have attended a small village public school with few books or other materials. They would have been expected to sit quietly in class and memorize information given by the teacher. Vietnamese students are not encouraged to look up information on their own or ask questions the way American students are.

In Chicago, Tu, Tuan, and Tuyen go to a large public school near their apartment. (Loan will start school when she is four years old.) The students come from many different backgrounds and speak many different languages.

At first, part of Tuan and Tu's school time was spent with a Vietnamese teacher, Miss Le, and other Vietnamese children. Miss Le helped to teach them English and to introduce them to American customs. She had come to America with her sister several years before the Nguyens. She had learned English in Vietnam. Her father was an official in the South Vietnamese government when the Communists took over. He was lucky to escape before they could arrest him.

Now Tu and Tuan spend more time in a regular classroom. They like math best of all, and they are good at it, too. Being with other American children helps them learn English more quickly. They have many more books and supplies than they would have had in Vietnam. And here they have a school library, assembly programs, and extracurricular activities, which students do not have in Vietnam.

Tuyen is in a Headstart program for preschool children. Music is her favorite subject, especially when she gets to lead the rhythm band.

Although they come from many different backgrounds, the children at the Nguyens' school enjoy playing together. In the picture, they are playing "Chinese jump rope." They've tied long rubber bands together and made them into a triangle. The point of the game is to jump in and out of the triangle without missing a step.

The games have different names than the ones children play in Vietnam, but they are played mostly the same way.

24

There were many more things to adjust to in the United States. Chicago's weather is different from the weather the Nguyens were used to. The southern part of Vietnam has a tropical climate. There it is hot and humid, and it never gets cold. Chicago winters are often cold and snowy. Before coming to the United States, the Nguyen children had never seen snow. The first time they saw it, they could hardly wait to touch it. Soon they were running and playing in the snow like other children.

For the first time, the Nguyens had to wear heavy coats and hats.

In Vietnam, people wear light cotton clothing to stay cool. Men wear lightweight pants and shirts. Women usually wear black slacks and short white jackets to work. To dress up they wear *ao dai*. These are high-necked, long-sleeved dresses that are slit up to the waist and worn with long, pajamalike pants. Girls and women are used to having their legs, arms, and necks covered.

The girls in the picture are wearing ao dai. They join Tuan and other Vietnamese classmates in singing and dancing to traditional Vietnamese music for a school assembly program.

Many foods were new and different, too. But the children soon learned to like hamburgers, pizza, hot dogs, and chocolate chip cookies!

Rice is the basic food of the Vietnamese. Many Vietnamese families in Uptown buy large sacks of rice because they use so much, and it costs less in large amounts. Fresh, uncooked vegetables are also an important part of the Vietnamese diet. The Vietnamese eat many salads. Another basic food is fish, which they eat more often than meat. Pork is the cheapest and most popular meat. They do not use as much milk, butter, or cheese as Americans.

The favorite sauce of the Vietnamese is a yellowy liquid made from anchovies and salt. It is used in cooking just about every Vietnamese dish. Mixed with crushed garlic, lemon juice, chili pepper, water, and sugar, it makes *nuoc cham*, which is served at almost every Vietnamese meal as a seasoning sauce.

The Vietnamese eat more fruits than sweets. Bananas, mangoes, papayas, oranges, coconuts, and pineapples are favorites. Sweets are usually eaten only on holidays or other special occasions.

Tea is the favorite drink of the Vietnamese. It is served before and after meals or with snacks. The Vietnamese often drink tea that has been mixed with dried flowers such as roses, jasmine, or chrysanthemums.

At first the Nguyens enjoyed shopping in the large supermarkets in Chicago, with so many products they had never seen before. Then they heard about a shopping area known as "Little Saigon" on nearby Argyle Street. Here are smaller Vietnamese and other Asian food stores, clothing shops, restaurants, and offices. There are signs the Nguyens can read, foods they are used to eating, and storekeepers who speak Vietnamese. On Sunday afternoons the whole Nguyen family likes to shop on Argyle Street.

Other things are different in America, too. In the school lunchroom the children use forks, knives, spoons, and sometimes their fingers. Most of the food is served on plates.

At home, as in Vietnam, the family mostly use chopsticks, or *duas*, for eating. And food is eaten out of bowls. The two chopsticks are held with three fingers of one hand and the small bowl with the other hand.

Not all things changed for the Nguyen family and their Vietnamese neighbors. As they did in Vietnam, they believe strong family ties will last forever. Children sing a song about love for their family. "We will honor Father and Mother, who take care of us," it says. "Father's work and devotion to the child is as great and high as a mountain. Mother's caring is like the gentle flow of water from the source."

Older people are greatly respected by the Vietnamese. When parents are old, children take care of them to show thanks for raising them. Family loyalty puts strong pressure on each member of the family. Children are taught to be careful of their actions because any mischief they do is blamed on the family. A Vietnamese proverb says, "A drop of blood is better than an ocean of water." It reminds people of the importance of family blood ties.

People who are dead are still thought of as important members of the family. Each family sets aside special "memory days" to honor the spirits of dead relatives. Memory days are often held on an ancestor's birthday or on the anniversary of the day the relative died.

In the pictures, the Nguyen family honors Mr. Nguyen's father, who died after the family left Vietnam.

They have made their mantel into an altar. On it are placed his picture and his favorite food—fresh fruit—and his favorite drink—Coca Cola. Candles are lit, and incense is burned. Then prayers are said for him and other dead relatives.

When the ceremony is over, the Nguyens sit down around the table and enjoy a meal of egg rolls, noodles, salad, and nuoc cham. They believe their observance of memory days strengthens their family ties.

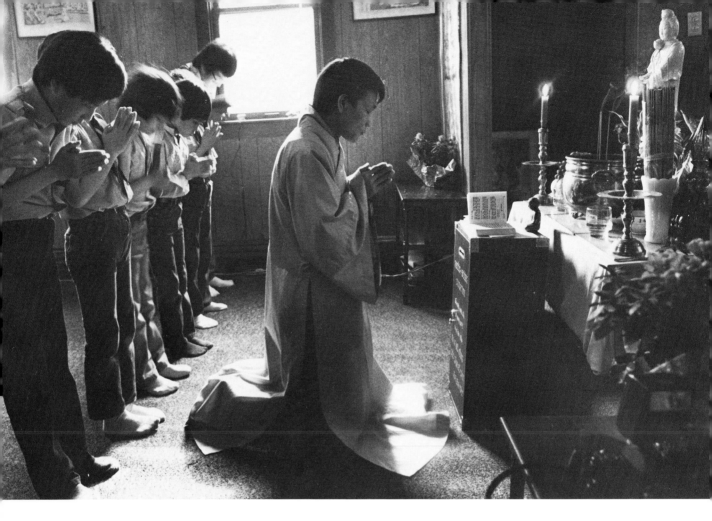

Some Vietnamese are Christians, including many who are Roman Catholics. But most Vietnamese are Buddhists.

Buddhism teaches people how to improve themselves and live peacefully with others. It encourages people to be kind rather than selfish and to be modest rather than boastful.

Buddhism was founded many centuries ago in India. The man who founded it was named Buddha, or the "Enlightened One," by his followers. Buddhists believe that if they follow the path of Buddha, they will find truth and perfect happiness.

The Vietnamese Buddhist Temple in Chicago is not like the beautiful temples of Vietnam. It is an old house that was made into a place of worship through the hard work of the Vietnamese people who attend services there. They hope, one day, to have enough money to build a beautiful temple like the ones they knew in Vietnam.

Those who attend the Sunday ceremony leave their shoes at the door before entering the temple. Inside is an altar with the Buddha's statue, lighted candles, and burning incense. On the walls hang many pictures showing the life and teachings of Buddha.

Courtesy of Trang Ton

The most important holiday of the year for the Vietnamese is Tet. Tet begins on the first day of the lunar new year. (The Vietnamese calendar differs from the calendar used in the United States. The Vietnamese measure time according to the lunar cycle—the cycle of the moon—not the sun.) It usually comes in the month of February and lasts for three days. Tet is a new year's celebration, a spring festival, a family reunion, and a national holiday all at the same time. It is a time of rebirth—a time to forget past mistakes, pardon others, correct all faults, and pay debts. Owing money during the holiday is thought to be bad luck. It is said that the Vietnamese have two birthdays every year. One is the date of their birth, and the other is Tet.

40

On the evening before Tet begins, a special ceremony is held in the home. Ancestors are invited to come back to join in celebrating the holiday. At midnight firecrackers are set off to welcome in the new year. In the morning, children are given red envelopes filled with money to buy toys and candy. People visit friends and relatives. Many Vietnamese believe that the first visitor received during the Tet holiday will influence their luck throughout the new year. Often they will invite the guest of their choice, to be safe.

Throughout the joyous holiday, people dress up in brightly colored clothing to celebrate. They also serve brightly colored foods. One of the most popular dishes is *banh Tet*. This is a cake made of rice, beans, pepper, nuoc mam, and pork wrapped in banana leaves. The leaves turn the rice cakes green. Some people serve pigs roasted until they are a deep, rich red. And colorful fruits—tangerines, grapefruits, and watermelon—are also eaten.

Often during the Tet festivities, the dragon dance is performed. The dragon has special significance to the Vietnamese. In fact, they are sometimes called the "children of the dragon." A favorite old fairytale tells how they got this name and how Vietnam began long, long ago. Once, the story goes, a kind, brave dragon wandered out of China and walked south until he came to a beautiful, warm land with high mountains, rivers of clear water, and rich soil in which fruit trees and wild rice grew in abundance.

After a while, the dragon became lonely. Then one day a beautiful fairy princess came down from the heavens. The dragon fell in love with her. They married and had a hundred children. Eventually the parents went away to live together in the spirit world. Their children and grandchildren and great-grandchildren all grew up to be as brave and kind as the dragon and as beautiful as the princess. The land where they lived became known as Vietnam.

Another holiday is the Vietnamese Children's Day, or Trung Thu, which comes at the time of the harvest moon. It is also known as the Mid-Autumn Festival. On this special day, children are honored. They are reminded to be good citizens and to have love and respect for one another and for their country.

Everyone eats moon cakes on Children's Day. These cakes are made of sticky rice filled with such things as peanuts, lotus seeds, duck-egg yolks, raisins, watermelon seeds, and tangerine peels.

At night, children march through the streets holding lighted lanterns as drums and cymbals are played. Sometimes the lanterns are in the shapes of boats, dragons, horses, and toads. The Vietnamese children in Uptown carry on this tradition by staging a parade every year. The dragon dance is often performed at this special time as well as during Tet.

Courtesy of Trang Ton

43

The Nguyen family know they must change to adapt to life in their new country. They must learn to speak English and find a new way of earning a living. But Mr. and Mrs. Nguyen hope their children will always have a love of family, respect for older people, and a high regard for education. The family must sort out which parts of their old customs they will keep and which they must change to fit into the American way of life. This takes time.

The Nguyens often think about their relatives in Vietnam and about their ancestors who are buried there. But they have started to adjust to a new life in the United States. The children are doing well in school. Mr. Nguyen is studying to be an automobile mechanic. He hopes to have a shop of his own someday. And Mrs. Nguyen will continue taking care of the family.

They probably always will observe Tet, the Vietnamese Children's Day, and their own special memory days. But now there are new holidays for them to celebrate such as Thanksgiving and the Fourth of July. The children especially enjoy dressing up in costumes for Halloween.

The Nguyen children, like their parents, are proud and happy to say, "America is our home and our country, too."

A Simple Pronunciation Guide to the Vietnamese Words and Names in This Book

ao dai (ow yeye)
banh Tet (bahn Teht)
dua (doo-uh)
Giao Kim (Zow Kihm)
hoa (hwah, said in a normal, even tone)
hòa (hwah, said in a low, falling tone)
Miss Le (Miss Lay)
Loan (Lwahn, rhymes with *swan*)
Nguyen (Noo-yehn)

nuoc cham (nuk chahm)
nuoc mam (nuk mahm)
Tet (Teht)
Tuyen Thanh (Too-yehn Tahn)
Trung thu (Chuhng thoo)
Tu Anh (Too Ahn)
Tuan Anh (Twahn Ahn)
Vietnam (Vee eht NAHM)
Xuan Thanh (Swahn Tahn)